$ 6

Story Adaptations by Etta Wilson
Illustrations by Bob Singer
Art Direction by Linda Karl

MALLARD PRESS
An Imprint of BDD Promotional Book Company, Inc.
666 Fifth Avenue
New York, N.Y. 10103

"Mallard Press and its accompanying design and logo
are trademarks of BDD Promotional Book Company, Inc."

Story Adaptations by March Media, Inc.
Illustrations by Singer/Bandy Group
Produced by Hamilton Projects, Inc.

ISBN 0-792-45155-4

Printed in the United States

MALLARD
PRESS

It was a grey misty morning and George Jetson was catching a few extra winks — until Rosie the robot maid rolled in. With a few clicks of her control rod, the lights came on, the drapes opened, and George's bed popped him out on the floor.

"Up and at 'em, Mr. J," she said.

3

George stepped on the people-mover track. In two minutes he had been showered, dried, toothbrushed, combed, and dressed. Rosie gave him a cube of toast for breakfast, and he was ready to leave for work.

"Have a good day, Dad," said Elroy.
"Love you, Dad," said Judy.
"Bye, dear," said Jane.
"I ruv you, Rorge," said Astro.
"I know, I know. I love you too!" George wiped his face and
   headed down the exit tube.

After a quick flight in his jetcar, George slid to his desk at Spacely Sprockets. One push of the button and his work was done. Then it was time to report in.

"This is George Jetson," he said to the speaker phone. "What's our old penny-pinching, pea-headed president up to today?"

"Mr. Spacely is meeting with the Board of Directors for the entire day," replied the voice on the phone.

That was George's signal. He leaned back to sleep — for the entire day.

In the board room, Mr. Spacely was telling the Board about his top secret project — the Orbiting Ore Asteroid Manufacturing Plant Unlimited International, Inc. — O.O.A.M.P.U.I.I. for short!

"This new plant on the asteroid produces sprockets at one-tenth of what it costs here," he said. "Soon we will produce our one-millionth sprocket in space!"

The Board cheered Spacely's news.

Just then Mr. Spacely got a call in his office from the robot manager at the asteroid plant. It was bad news! Another vice president had left and there was no one to push the start button. Spacely was worried. He had promised the Board more money from the new plant, but it kept breaking down.

"What I need is someone who is loyal, follows my instructions, works cheap — and can push a button! That's it — Jetson!" He called George to his office. When George whizzed through the door, Spacely greeted him with a big smile.

"Welcome aboard, Vice President Jetson!"

"Me? Vice President? George was dazed.

"I knew you were the right man for the job up there! With your family beside you, you face a new challenge — a new button to push — in space!"

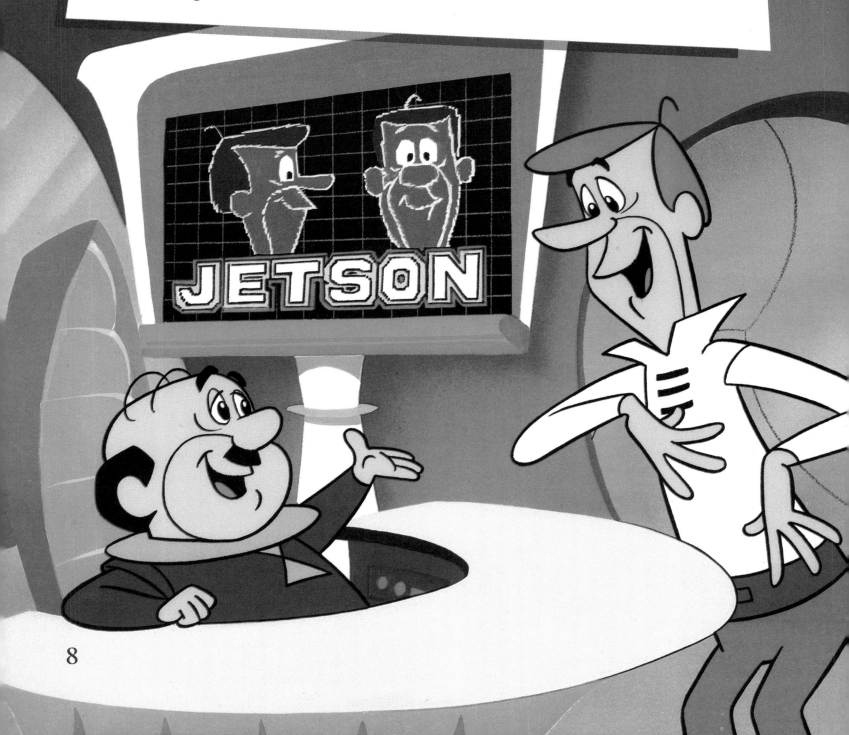

At Elroy's school, the basketball game was all tied up. The coach looked down the bench and called Elroy to go in.

"Shall I give 'em the Elroy Elevator shot, Coach?"

"What else? It's the only shot you got! Get out there and sink it!"

Elroy dribbled and faked. "Going up, Going down! Going up! Going down! Going in!"

But the ball didn't go in and the game ended! Elroy's team lost!

"My life is over!" Elroy cried as he left the gym alone.

9

Meanwhile, Judy had joined her friends at the teen hangout to dance to the music of their favorite rock singer — Cosmic Cosmo. Suddenly Cos came over to dance with Judy.

"Hey, what's your name?" he asked.

"Ju-Ju-Judy," she stammered.

"Well, Ju-Ju-Judy, we've got a date Friday night!"

Judy squealed with delight. "Imagine! A date with Cosmic Cosmo!"

George had big news for the family when he got home that night. "They made me a vice president! We're moving to Spacely's Orbiting Ore Asteroid — tomorrow!"

"Move? But, George, I'm redecorating here," said Jane.

"But, Daddy, I've got a date with Cosmic Cosmo!" cried Judy.

"I'll start packing!" said Elroy.

"Hey, I thought you'd be happy," said George. "I'm a vice president!"

"Maybe it won't be so bad, dear," Jane said.

Early the next day, the Jetsons were zooming off to their new home on the asteroid.

"There it is!" yelled Elroy.

"Look, Judy, it's got a shopping mall!" Jane said.

"And there's the new plant!" said George.

"*Your* new plant, Mr. Vice President!" Jane replied.

When the Jetsons walked into their new apartment, they found—nothing! It was empty and bare.

"Where's my room?" asked Elroy.

"Where's the phone!" asked Judy.

"I wonder if this thing works up here," Rosie said as she held up her control rod and clicked it a few times.

Things started to happen fast. Lights came on, beds shot out of the wall, a complete kitchen rolled in — even a telephone flipped down for Judy!

"Oh, wow! This is nebular!"

Just then the doorbell rang. It was Lucy 2, their new neighbor.
"You'll meet my husband, Rudy 2, at the plant. And we have
a son, Teddy 2. We were built as a complete family unit," she said.
"I want to show you around the mall tomorrow."
Life on the asteroid was looking better all the time!

Later that day Elroy brought home a strange new pet. George and Jane were trying to decide who he might belong to when two large creatures just like the little one appeared at the door.

"We're the Furbelows, Bertie, Gertie, and that's our little Fergee. She's a girl. We live next door."

"We're pleased to meet you," Jane replied.

It was quiet that night at the orbiting ore plant until, all at once, there were little sounds like the scratching of mice feet and tiny beams of light in the dark shadows. . .

George arrived at the plant for his first day as vice president early the next morning.

"What a place!" he said to the robot man who met him there. "You must be Rudy! I want to meet all the employees right away."

"You just did," said Rudy 2. "It's all in your hands — or should I say finger?"

Rudy took George high above the plant to show him how it worked.

"There's the drilling bore. It brings up the ore," he said to George.

"The bore brings up the ore. Got it," replied George.

"The ore makes the sprockets. We pack the sprockets into packets and sack the packets into brackets for the lockers."

"Do you lock the sprocket packets in the bracket lockers?" asked George.

"Right," said Rudy, "and you keep the sprocket locker key in the pocket to your jacket — until we take the bored ore sprocket packets and rocket the sprockets to Spacely!"

"You've done everything!" George said.

"Everything but press the button that gets it going — that's your job, George."

"Just tell me when you're ready!"

Meanwhile Lucy 2 was showing Jane and Judy the asteroid mall. "Here we are — the Galaxy Galleria!"

Judy was impressed. "I'd sort of like to wander around by myself," she said.

"Go ahead, dear," said Jane. "Just be back in time for us to get to the plant for Dad's big button pushing."

Judy was scooting down the spiral elevator on her floating disc, trying to see as much as she could. But she didn't see the boy up ahead until she smashed into him!

"Ow! you dum — duhhh!" She stopped for a closer look.

"Dummy?" he asked with a laugh. "Actually, my name's Apollo Blue."

"I'm Judy. Oh, I've got to go. It's two minutes to twelve."

"See you tomorrow, pumpkin. Same time, same place?" Apollo called.

At Elroy's school on the asteroid, the boys played basketball much like they did on earth. The coach paired Elroy against Teddy 2 for some one-on-one.

"My name may be Teddy 2, but I'm number one in this game," he said to Elroy.

"You mean you *were* number one. Watch my elevator shot!"

Elroy dribbled and faked. "Going up! Going down! Going up! Going down! Going in!"

"No way!" yelled Teddy 2 as his mechanical arm zoomed out to catch the ball.

Elroy was stunned!

"Coming to the ceremony at the plant?" asked Teddy 2.

"You bet!" replied Elroy.

Everyone was at the plant at noon. George stood at the control panel ready to push the button and make the millionth sprocket on the orbiting ore asteroid plant.

Mr. Spacely and the Board were watching from earth.

"Okay, Jetson, push the button!" called Spacely.

The sprocket counter read 999,998 and then 999,999. . .

"Here it comes! One million sprockets!" yelled George.

Suddenly a sprocket went sailing past George's head. The counter started going backwards. Then sprockets started flying all around. George tried to catch the flying sprockets, but they were coming too fast! Elroy saw one of them hit Teddy 2 and raced over to help him up. Then Rudy 2 hurried the families out of the plant.

"Jetson, you're destroying my plant! Turn that machine off!" yelled Spacely.

"Yes sir! Right away, sir!"

"And get it started soon! Lost time means lost vice presidents!"

Back at the Jetsons' apartment the two families were treating their wounds after the disaster. Rudy 2 tried to explain to George that strange things kept happening at the plant.

"You mean they're not accidents?" asked George.

"No, they were a warning — to close the plant down. That's why Spacely's had four vice presidents. They all had accidents like today — and left!"

"Well, I'm not leaving!" George said. "If someone's sneaking in at night to foul things up, I'm going back tonight and keep watch! George Jetson is taking charge!"

Elroy and Teddy 2 were now best friends. As they heard their dads talking, Elroy had an idea.

The plant was dark that night when George returned.

"All right, you vandals, now you've got George Jetson to deal with!"

George searched the plant high and low with his flashlight and then sat down at his desk to wait. He was soon sound asleep.

The skittering and scurrying of little feet didn't wake him—
even when the little creatures carried him off in the dark.

"My Dad needs help," Elroy said to Teddy 2. "I'm going to the plant and help him solve the mystery of those accidents. All I need is my detecto kit."

"And me," said Teddy 2. "With my elevator shot, we can go through the vent into the plant."

"Wow! Let's go!" Elroy said with a laugh. "Going up! Going up! Going in!"

As the boys slipped inside, they surprised the little creatures in the dark. Elroy's flashlight passed over them quickly.

"Squeep! Shh!" They scurried off — all except one!

"What was that noise?" asked Elroy.

"Look! Those buckets are moving!"

Each of the boys snatched up a bucket. Under one they found Fergee Furbelow, who pointed to the creature under the other and said, "Grunchee!"

The little Grunchee hopped up on the bucket and began to explain some things.

"Grunchee deedle de dum de… WHAM! Whee! Whaaa! Whump!"

"I'm programmed for most languages," said Teddy 2, "and I can tell you that the Grunchee people are not very happy with us. His name is Squeep, and he says we've been destroying their town with the orbiting ore drill."

"My dad wouldn't do that! I want to see for myself!"

Squeep thought for a second, then nodded and pointed toward the buckets on the ore machine that went below the plant floor.

"Elroy Jetson!" Judy called.

She and Apollo had come looking for the boys when Jane discovered they were not at home asleep.

"Well, Well! What have we got here?" asked Apollo.

"He's a Grunchee," said Elroy. "And he's going to show us why the plant keeps having accidents. Come with us, will you, guys?"

"Let's go!" Apollo helped Judy into one of the buckets.

Slowly the bucket went down into the dark center of the asteroid.
"Teddy, are you programmed to be scared?" Elroy asked.
"No."
"I am!" said Elroy.

As the bucket stopped on the cavern floor, the kids saw
hundreds of tiny lights go on in the dark shadows. The entire cavern
was full of Grunchees! And they were all looking at the kids
in the bucket!

Squeep hopped out quickly and led the rest of them across the cavern through the maze of Grunchee homes.

Judy was looking straight ahead.

"Oh, no!" she exclaimed, "We're destroying their homes!"

The sharp point of the huge drill from the plant above had bored through the ceiling. Piles of rocks and ore had crashed into some of the homes. It was a sad sight.

Up in the plant, Jane, Rudy 2, and Astro had come to look for George and the boys. Astro sniffed for familiar smells near the shaft.

"Relroy! Rorge!" He barked and jumped into one of the ore buckets.

Jane joined him and the bucket went down to the cavern.

"There you are, Elroy Jetson," said Jane. "Now we've found everybody except George."

Suddenly George hopped into the cavern. His hands and feet were tied.

"George, what happened?" Jane peeled the tape off his mouth.

"I was kidnapped by those vicious little furballs!"

"Daddy, they were just trying to save their homes." Judy said.

"Um, George dear," said Jane, " I think we need to have a little talk before I untie you." Then Jane leaned over to whisper in George's ear.

"NO! NO! NO! NO! And that's final!"

"George, all I ask is that you look around and see what your job is making you do. No job is worth that."

Up above in the plant, there was a familiar yell. "Jetson! Jetson!"
Mr. Spacely had taken the first cheap flight to the asteroid.
"Why is this plant shut down?" he asked Rudy 2. "I want my one
millionth sprocket if I have to make it myself. The Board expects
more money!"

Before Rudy 2 could stop him, Spacely pushed the red button
on the control panel and the giant drill bit started to turn.

With each turn the drill dug deeper into the cavern below! The whole place began to rumble and shake. Cracks opened like an earthquake. Rocks fell and a huge chunk of ore broke away from the ceiling. Jane looked at the pile of rubble where Elroy and Squeep had been standing.

"Elroy!" she screamed.

"Squeep! Ibblroy! Wooooop! Ibbble! Grunchee!"

Quick as a wink, a group of Grunchees knew what to do. They formed a chain and burrowed into the rubble.

Elroy came out of the pile headfirst, and in his hand was little Squeep!

"Thanks! Thank you very much!" said George. "Come on, all of you. We've got work to do."

With everyone close behind him, George raced up to the plant control panel.

"What are you doing, Jetson?" yelled Spacely. "Stay away from that button!"

"No, sir, Mr. Spacely!" George leaned over and pushed the OFF button. "Did you know about those wonderful little creatures who live below the plant?" George saw the look on Spacely's face.

"Why, you money-grabbing old goat! You did know! Well, let me tell you, these creatures just saved my boy's life. They've got hearts. They care, but you wouldn't know about that, would you?"

"Stop it! Stop it! I can't stand any more!" said Spacely.

"Then figure a way to keep the plant and let the Grunchees have their homes too. It's the only way you'll ever get your millionth sprocket!"

45

The very next day everyone watched proudly as the Grunchees worked the sprocket machines. The sprockets came out sparkling and perfect. Best of all, the Grunchees' homes were safe.

"I don't believe it. They've doubled production!" said Rudy 2.
George watched the sprocket counter carefully.
"999,999. . . 1,000,000!"
Cheers and shouts rang through the plant.
"Jetson, it's time to plan your trip home. You've done enough here," said Spacely.
"Yes sir, Mr. Spacely, but will I be a vice president?"
"Oh, all right! But no raise!"

The Jetsons were soon headed home to earth in their jetcar. With many hugs, promises to visit and a few tears, they said good-bye to all their new friends on the asteroid. As the car pulled out into space, Elroy looked back.

"Look, Dad! It's the Grunchees on the roof of our apartment!"

And there they were — waving and flashing their lights and calling, "Thanks, George."

"Well, that sure is nice of them," George said as he blinked a tear from his eye.